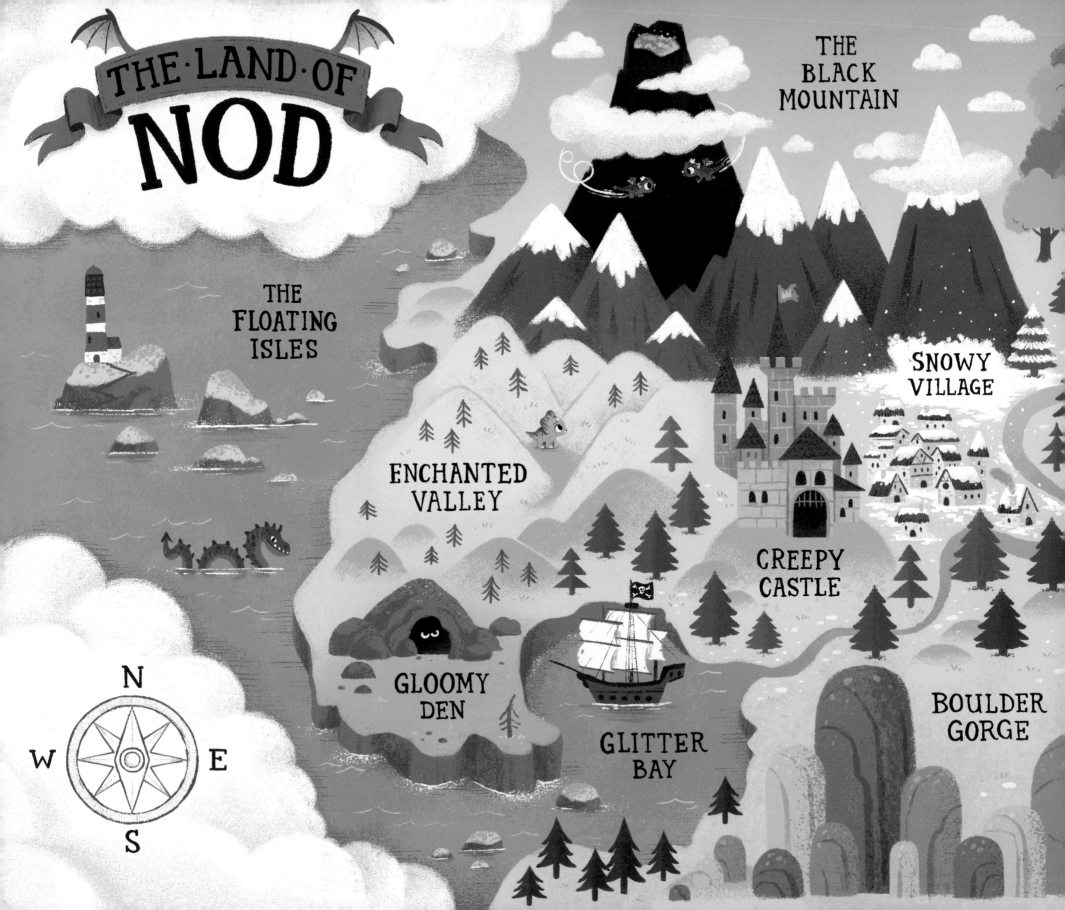

For Megan
R.F.

For Milo
C.C.

LADYBIRD BOOKS

UK | USA | Canada | Ireland | Australia | India | New Zealand | South Africa
Ladybird Books is part of the Penguin Random House group of companies
whose addresses can be found at global.penguinrandomhouse.com.
www.penguin.co.uk   www.puffin.co.uk   www.ladybird.co.uk

First published 2021
001
Written by Rhiannon Fielding. Text copyright © Ladybird Books Ltd, 2021
Illustrations copyright © Chris Chatterton, 2021
Moral rights asserted
Printed in China
The authorized representative in the EEA is Penguin Random House Ireland,
Morrison Chambers, 32 Nassau Street, Dublin D02 YH68
A CIP catalogue record for this book is available from the British Library
ISBN: 978–0–241–46437–3
All correspondence to:
Ladybird Books, Penguin Random House Children's
One Embassy Gardens, 8 Viaduct Gardens
London SW11 7BW

MIX
Paper from
responsible sources
FSC
www.fsc.org   FSC® C018179

TEN MINUTES TO BED

Little Dragon

Rhiannon Fielding • Chris Chatterton

Above a black mountain that towers so high,
bright jets of flame burst and light up the sky.
Ten minutes to bed! The air hums with a sound,
and the soft thud of beating wings echoes around.

Everywhere, dragons! Look out below!
They **zoom** through the sky in a fiery red glow.
It's **nine minutes to bedtime,** and no one flies quicker

than one little **mischievous** dragon called **Flicker.**

Speeding along,
Flicker soared
and he **swooped** –
he flew through the sky in a huge
loop-the-loop!

"I'll race you!" he called to his big sister, Flash.

"Eight minutes to bed,
so you'd better not crash!"

The other young dragons
were all **well behaved.**
Seven minutes! They flew home
to nest in their caves.

But in all the commotion,
not one of them spied . . .

an egg rolling fast down the steep mountainside.

Flicker and Flash were **not** ready for bed.
"A little bit further! Six minutes," they said.

Darting and diving,
they laughed as they flew –

two streaks of colour that burst through the blue.

In the distance,
a rainbow shone bright in the sky.
"A unicorn wish!" whispered Flash with a sigh.
"Five minutes to bed:
we should turn back around . . ."

But her brother
had seen something
down on the ground.

With a *whoosh!* Flicker landed,

his small wings spread wide.

Flash followed him, tiptoeing close by his side.

On the ground lay an egg

that shone purple and black . . .

and as Flicker watched it,
it started to crack.

Sniffing it gently,

he nudged with his nose –

the lost egg rolled forward

and stopped by his toes.

"Four minutes," said Flash.

"Can you carry it, Flicker?"

He smiled.

"There's no other dragon
who's quicker!"

He **picked up the egg,** and then – taking great care –
Flicker **launched himself** upwards, back into the air.
Three minutes to bed: the sky had grown dark,

but Flash lit their way

with a **shower**

of **sparks.**

Soon, flying swiftly, the two dragons saw
the distant black mountain, and far-off seashore.
"Two minutes to bed," said a bird as it passed.

"You're nearly back home . . .
but that egg's hatching fast!"

They **settled the egg** on a small pile of leaves,
where a **big** mummy dragon looked very relieved.

Crack!

First a wing . . .

then a tail . . .

then a horn . . .

The new **baby dragon** emerged with a yawn.

Flicker and Flash crept back home to their nest.
One minute to bed, and at last – time to rest!
They stretched out their wings, and they snuggled up tight . . .

and soon they were soaring through
soft starlit night.

THE·LAND·OF NOD

THE BLACK MOUNTAIN

THE FLOATING ISLES

SNOWY VILLAGE

ENCHANTED VALLEY

CREEPY CASTLE

GLOOMY DEN

GLITTER BAY

BOULDER GORGE

N
W   E
S

THE
ANCIENT FOREST

OUTER
SPACE

EMERALD
GLEN

DEADLY
CREEK

GIANTS' TOWN

RICKETY
BRIDGE

THE
STINKY
SWAMPS

GOLDEN
COVE

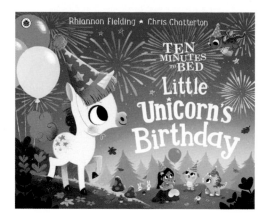

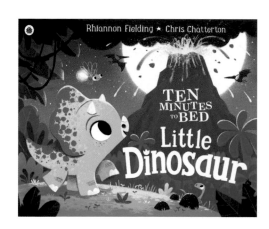

Look out for more
bedtime adventures in

THE·LAND·OF
NOD

Have you met **Twinkle** the unicorn, **Belch** the monster,
Splash the mermaid and **Rumble** the dinosaur?